Scholastic
Clifford
THE
BIG EGG HUNT

Written by Suzanne Weyn

Illustrated by Jim Durk

Based on the Scholastic book series "Clifford The Big Red Dog" by Norman Bridwell

Cartwheel B·O·O·K·S ®

SCHOLASTIC INC.

New York   Toronto   London   Auckland   Sydney   Mexico City
New Delhi   Hong Kong   Buenos Aires

ISBN 0-439-33246-X

Library of Congress Cataloging-in-Publication Data available

10 9 8 7 6 5 4 3 2 1   02 03 04 05 06

Printed in the U.S.A.   24
First printing, March 2002

It was the day of the big

Kids and Pups Egg Hunt.

"Remember the rules,"

said Sheriff Lewis.

"The pups find the eggs.

The kids pick them up."

"Go!" said Sheriff Lewis.

Charley went with T-Bone.

Vaz went with Cleo.

Jetta went with Mac.

And Emily Elizabeth went with Clifford.

The dogs sniffed and sniffed.

Clifford was the first to find some eggs.

They were high up in a tree.

"Woof!" he barked.

Emily Elizabeth giggled.

"We can't take these eggs.

They belong to Mama Robin!"

T-Bone saw an egg

under a bench.

But before he had a chance to bark,

Cleo barked first.

And Vaz picked up the egg.

Then T-Bone saw an egg

on the slide.

But before he had a chance to bark,

Clifford barked first.

And Emily Elizabeth picked up the egg.

T-Bone saw an egg

behind a rock.

But before he had a chance to bark,

Mac barked first.

And Jetta picked up the egg.

After a while,

everyone had lots of eggs—

everyone but T-Bone and Charley.

They didn't have any.

"I have no luck,"

T-Bone said to Clifford.

"You can have some of my eggs,"

said Clifford.

"No, thanks," T-Bone said.

"I want to find the eggs myself."

Then Clifford had an idea.

He told it to Cleo and Mac.

"Let's hide some of our eggs

where T-Bone can find them,"

said Clifford.

Mac didn't like the idea.

He didn't think it was fair.

"But it would make T-Bone so happy,"

said Cleo. "And Charley, too!"

"Oh, all right," said Mac.

"How will we get the kids

to help us out?" Cleo asked.

"Just watch me," said Clifford.

Clifford walked over to Emily Elizabeth.

He carefully tipped over her basket.

And one of the eggs fell out.

Clifford rolled the egg

into the tall grass!

T-Bone found it right away!

"Woof!" he barked.

And Charley picked it up.

Cleo walked over to Vaz.

She carefully tipped over his basket.

And one of the eggs fell out.

Cleo rolled it over to a tree.

T-Bone found that one, too!

"Woof!" T-Bone barked.

And Charley picked it up.

Then Mac tipped over

Jetta's basket.

He rolled one of his eggs

toward some vines.

"Woof!" T-Bone barked.

And Charley picked up the egg.

Soon T-Bone and Charley

had as many eggs as their friends.

"You have lots of eggs now,"

Clifford said to T-Bone.

"You *are* lucky, after all!"

"I am lucky," said T-Bone,

"but not because I found these eggs.

I know what you guys did.

You put these eggs

where I could find them.

I'm lucky because I have good friends

who want me to be happy.

Thanks, guys!"

So everyone ate eggs—

and everyone was happy!

Do You Remember?

Circle the right answer.
1. Which dog is the first to find eggs?
   a. T-Bone
   b. Cleo
   c. Clifford

2. T-Bone says he is lucky because…
   a. he found many eggs.
   b. he has good friends.
   c. he ate many eggs.

Which happened first?
Which happened next?
Which happened last?
Write a 1, 2, or 3 in the space after each sentence.

T-Bone saw an egg behind a rock. _____

Cleo tipped over Vaz's basket. _____

Clifford found eggs in a robin's nest. _____

Answers:
Clifford found eggs in a robin's nest. (1)
Cleo tipped over Vaz's basket. (3)
T-Bone saw an egg behind a rock. (2)
2. b
1. c